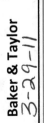

MISS DOROTHY

and

HER BOOKMOBILE

By Gloria Houston · *Illustrated by* Susan Condie Lamb

HARPER

An Imprint of HarperCollinsPublishers

Miss Dorothy and Her Bookmobile

Text copyright © 2011 by Gloria Houston

Illustrations copyright © 2011 by Susan Condie Lamb

All rights reserved. Manufactured in China. No part of this book may be
used or reproduced in any manner whatsoever without written permission
except in the case of brief quotations embodied in critical articles and
reviews. For information address HarperCollins Children's Books,
a division of HarperCollins Publishers, 10 East 53rd Street,
New York, NY 10022. www.harpercollinschildrens.com

Library of Congress Cataloging-in-Publication Data is available.

ISBN 978-0-06-029155-6 (trade bdg.)

ISBN 978-0-06-029156-3 (lib. bdg.)

Typography by Sarah Hoy

11 12 13 14 15 SCP 10 9 8 7 6 5 4 3 2 1

❖

First Edition

For all Librarians, who bring
the world to our door(s)
—G.H.

To Clara Church Cohen
—S.C.L.

When Dorothy was a young girl,
she loved books,
and she loved people,
so she decided
that she would become a librarian.
She would be in charge
of a fine brick library
just like the one where she checked out books
in the center of the town square
in her hometown in Massachusetts.

So she went to Radcliffe College,
where she read almost all the books
in the big school library.

Then she went to library school,
where she learned all the things
a good librarian should know.

Finally, one bright spring day,
Dorothy graduated,
ready to be a librarian
in a fine brick library
just like the one in the center of the square
in her hometown.

Soon, however,
Miss Dorothy fell in love
and got married.
Her new husband wanted to move to a farm
in a land she had only seen on maps
but had read about in books,
a land of high blue mountains,
with deep green valleys
and cascading streams
splashing silver,
shaded with oak, maple, and fir,

at the base of high Mount Mitchell
in the Blue Ridge Mountains
of North Carolina.

The land was lovely there,
and Miss Dorothy's garden grew lush and tall.
Out in the fields
wildflowers bloomed
red, yellow, blue, and gold.

Inside her cozy house,
Miss Dorothy read all the books on her shelves.
Her new friends and neighbors
brought their books to share,
just as they shared vegetables
from their bountiful gardens.
But there was no library.
And there was no place
for Miss Dorothy
to be a librarian.

Then one day a meeting was called
of all the friends who liked to read.
"We need a library
to store the books
and check them out,"
Miss Dorothy said.
Then Dr. Masters,
the eldest man in the community,
spoke.

"Once we had a rolling library here,"
he said.
"Dr. Wing, over at the boys' school,
shared his books by placing them
in every post office,
church, and store.
He took them from place to place
in wooden crates on an oxen wagon."
"A library is a building
with shelves and books
and windows,"
Miss Dorothy said sadly.
Mrs. Erickson, the music teacher,
took off her hat
and placed a dollar bill into it.
"This is to buy a bookmobile," she said.
Everyone placed
the money they could spare
into the hat,
and they all agreed
that Miss Dorothy would be the librarian.

Finally, the new green bookmobile arrived,
and everyone turned out to watch
as Miss Dorothy lifted the side panels
and propped them on supports
so the books were shaded from sun and rain.

Many of the people brought books
to Miss Dorothy's house,
and she stored them in her basement.
Every day
she struggled up and down the steep staircase,
her arms loaded with books
to line the shelves of the bookmobile.

And sitting straight and tall,
she drove the bookmobile
over high hills and through narrow valleys,

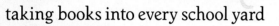
taking books into every school yard

and to visit every farm,

post office, grocery store,

churchyard,

and parking lot.

She stopped at the Tar Heel mica mill,
and she parked at the courthouse steps
at lunchtime
whenever court was in session.

If her readers could not come
to the bookmobile,
Miss Dorothy took books to them.
When elderly Mrs. Maumey
had read all her books,
she hung her husband's
red flannel drawers
on the line,
and Miss Dorothy climbed the hill
with more books to share
with her reading friend.

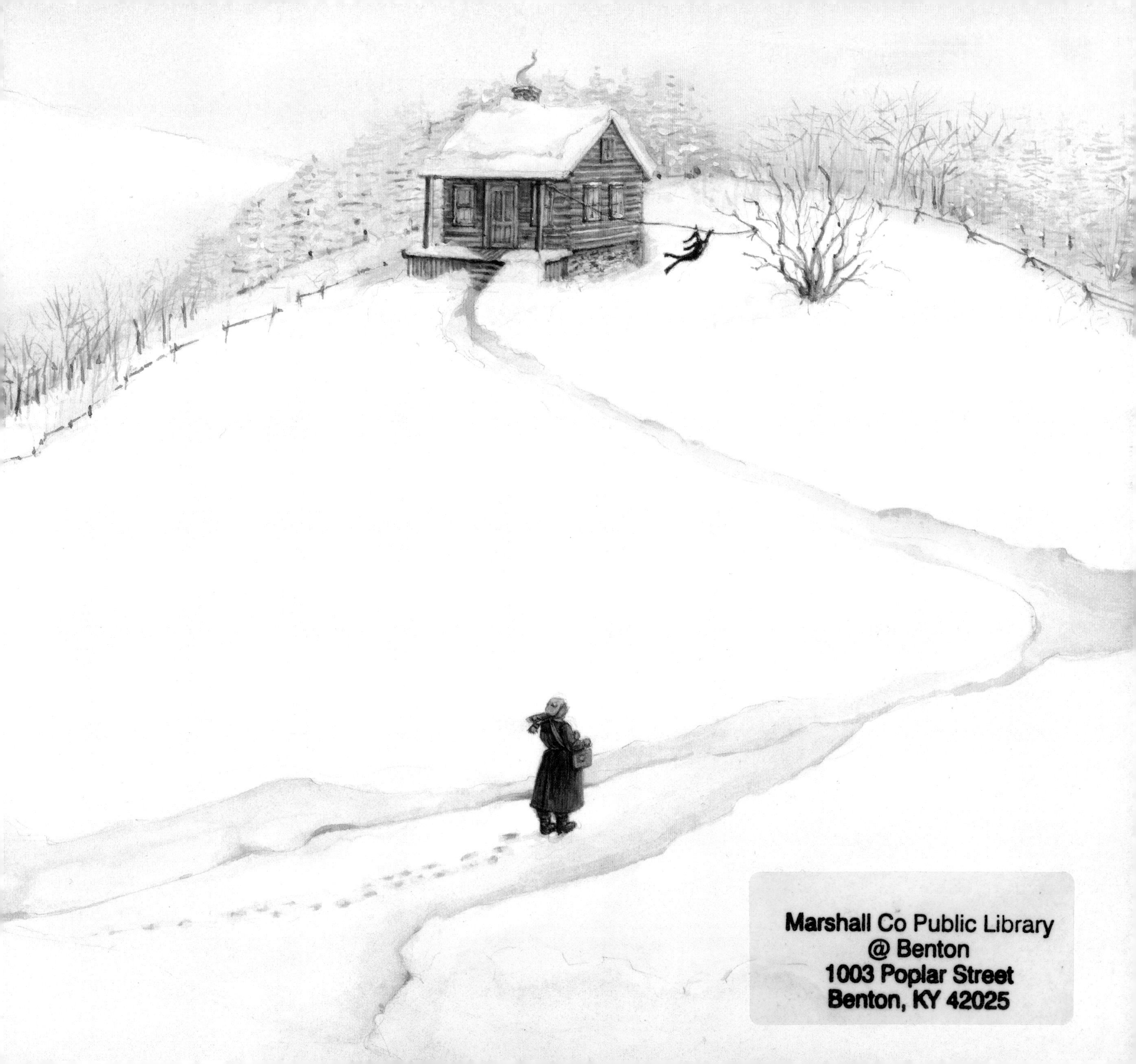

Soon everyone learned
that Miss Dorothy would check out books
wherever and whenever
she happened to be,
even in the middle
of the North Toe River.
The year the big rains made
the rivers into oceans of mud,
the embankments grew soft and slippery.
As she drove around the bend
in the River Road,
Miss Dorothy and the bookmobile
went slowly sliding
into the rushing waters below.
Miss Dorothy crawled out the window
to cling to the side of the van
until it came to rest
on an island.
"I thought I would be a real librarian,"
she told herself,
scraping mud from her skirt,
"in a fine brick library
in the center of town.
And just look at me now!"

Finally a farmer on his tractor
came down the road
and saw the bookmobile.
"Miss Dorothy," he called.
"Do you have a book of poems
I could borrow?"
"As soon as you help me upright the van,"
she answered.

When the bookmobile
was back on its wheels,
she opened the door,
swept out the mud,
straightened her hair, and,
with a smile,
she said,
"The library is open for business."

The students at Riverside School
stood waiting in line,
sun or rain,
for the little green bookmobile
to drive into the school yard,
its wheels scattering stones
at the side of the playground.

No one was more excited
to see Miss Dorothy
than one brown-eyed boy
named Ben,
who read every book about airplanes
and every volume of great adventures
Miss Dorothy could find.
"One day," he told her,
"I will go see the world
in these books
for myself."

Everywhere Miss Dorothy went,
she made new reading friends.
One of them
was a girl named Barbara,
who could not go to school.
She spent her days in a wheelchair
and had visited a hospital
in Massachusetts,
where she had seen
the fine brick library
in the center of Miss Dorothy's hometown.
Miss Dorothy brought her
stacks
and stacks
and stacks of books.
"You read them faster
than I can bring them,"
Miss Dorothy told her,
but she was smiling the broad smile
of a happy librarian,
who enjoys nothing so much
as sharing her books with her friends.

One day
a reader donated a little white house
to be used as a library.
"It will have to do."
Miss Dorothy sighed,
remembering the fine brick library
in her hometown.
Everyone showed up to clean and paint
until the new library
was ready to open.
The mothers baked cookies.
The fathers cut firewood
for the round black stove.
Students loaded the shelves
with books.
Mrs. Maumey sent her best lace tablecloth
and silver punch bowl,
and she offered
Mr. Maumey's red flannel drawers
for the flagpole, too.

The years came and went.
After a while,
awards covered Miss Dorothy's walls,
and people came from everywhere
to visit her library
and write articles about her
and her readers
in a land of high blue mountains,
with deep green valleys
and cascading streams
splashing silver.
Miss Dorothy rarely thought
of the fine brick library
in the center of the square
back home in Massachusetts.
She was far too busy
in her fine little library,
where people loved to read,
and where everyone loved Miss Dorothy.

Every day the mail truck brought letters
from Miss Dorothy's readers,
some nearby
and some very far away.
One of them came from Ben,
now a pilot in the U.S. Air Force.
He said,

You showed me the world
through books,
and now I have gone
to see it for myself.
Thank you
for being a librarian.

Another letter said,

Thank you
for loving books
and for loving people.
Although you were never in charge
of a fine brick library
like the one in your hometown,
  you are a real librarian.
    You have readers
      who love you
        and the books you share.
          Thank you
            for bringing the world
              to our door.

                Love, Barbara

AUTHOR'S NOTE

Dorothy Thomas was one of my heroes as a child. Her little green van with a fresh batch of books would arrive every two weeks at the store my family operated. During alternate weeks, she would drive into the school yard. I checked out new books from her every week!

The rural area where I lived had no library building, but residents there were avid readers. Mrs. Thomas stored the combined library collections of Avery, Mitchell, and Yancy Counties in her basement, carrying them up and down the stairs each morning and night. Many of my contemporaries from the area—including Ben Harding, James Byrd, and Barbara Davenport—have told me that she was one of the brightest spots in their lives. Everyone remembers the tiny woman with great fondness and how she touched their lives, though no one living today seems to know where she is buried. There is no monument to her—no stone with her name on it, that is. Her memorial is the love of books she engendered in the lives of her patrons, young and old.